tale New

... N... AND EVER...

...! ...

...OLF

...HTDRESS

IN BIG TROUBLE AGAIN!

...claims that it is quite usual for him to ...r these things while he is relaxing.

"There ain't no law that says a wolf ...can't wear a nightdress," he growled.

"I like pretty things. It's always the same. ...wolves get the blame for everything.

I've dun nuffin' wrong"

BB Wolf added that he is consulting his lawyers Tweedledum & Tweedledee about the unprovoked attack on his ...es. person by Mr Hood.

What a HOWLER! BB Wolf feels the long arm of the Law

KISS ME QUICK!

...OCKS

...a report that ...d a chair

...ttle Puddle Pond

EXC

Fairytale News

CHARLIE WAG ★ ★ FAIRYLAND'S TOP NEWSHOUND

For the arrival of Summer

First published 2004 by Walker Books Ltd
87 Vauxhall Walk, London SE11 5HJ

10 9 8 7 6 5 4 3 2

© 2004 Colin and Jacqui Hawkins

The right of Colin and Jacqui Hawkins to be identified as author
and illustrator respectively of this work has been asserted by them
in accordance with the Copyright, Designs and Patents Act 1988

This book has been typeset in Aunt Mildred

Printed in China

British Library Cataloguing in Publication Data:
a catalogue record for this book is available
from the British Library

ISBN 0-7445-9257-7

www.walkerbooks.co.uk

Fairytale News

Colin & Jacqui Hawkins

WALKER BOOKS
AND SUBSIDIARIES
LONDON • BOSTON • SYDNEY • AUCKLAND

Once upon a time, in an old tumbledown

cottage on the edge of Tangled Wood, lived
Mother Hubbard with her son, Jack.

One morning Mother Hubbard
went to the cupboard, but the
cupboard was bare.
"What shall we do?" she
cried. "We've no food and
no money. Jack, you'll have
to find a job or we'll starve."

We haven't got a bean.

Crumbs!

So Jack scooted off into town. He looked all over for work.

| He tried | Then he tried |
| PORKERS THE BUTCHERS. | WAX & WAYNE. |

Sorry, Jack.

Sorry, Jack.

SEE IN THE DARK
LIGHT A CANDLE

And then he tried
PAT-A-CAKE BAKERY.
Poor Jack couldn't
get a job anywhere.

Just then he saw a sign in the Tittle Tattle News
window, saying PAPERBOY/GIRL WANTED. APPLY WITHIN.
So in Jack rushed.

Mrs Tattle was delighted.
"The job's yours,"
she said, and gave
Jack a big bag of the
"Fairytale News"
to deliver.

Jack scurried off happily.
**"I'm going to be the
best paperboy ever!"** he said.

Jack's first delivery was to the home of the Three Bears,
who lived at Honey Cottage in Hickory Lane.

Inside Honey Cottage, the Three Bears were about to have breakfast when Jack popped the newspaper through the letterbox.

Mr Bear picked up the paper and sat down at the kitchen table.

"What's for breakfast, Mum?" asked Baby Bear.

"It's your favourite," said Mrs Bear.

"Porridge!" shouted Baby Bear.

One of the Little Pigs' houses has been blown down.

Mr Bear put down his paper and they all tucked into their porridge, but it was much too hot. "Never mind," said Mrs Bear. "Let's all go for a walk while it cools down." So, leaving the hot porridge to cool, the Three Bears set off for a walk in the woods.

Ow! Too hot!

Oh dear, that's the last straw.

They had not been gone two minutes, when the door of the cottage opened **and in came ...**

ZOOM!

Goldilocks!

Goldilocks was a very naughty little girl.

First she jumped on Mr Bear's big chair.

Next she jumped on Mrs Bear's middle-sized chair.

Then she jumped on Baby Bear's little chair and broke it!

Then Goldilocks spotted the Bears' breakfast on the table.

First she tried some of Mr Bear's porridge.

Next she tried Mrs Bear's porridge.

Then she tried Baby Bear's, and gobbled it all up!

All the porridge-tasting made Goldilocks feel very sleepy, so she went upstairs to have a nap.

First she got into Mr Bear's big bed.

Next she got into Mrs Bear's middle-sized bed.

Finally she snuggled into Baby Bear's little bed.

"Perfect," said Goldilocks, and she instantly fell into a deep, deep sleep.

Meanwhile, further up the road, Jack delivered a copy of the "Fairytale News" to Woodbine Cottage.

This was the cosy home
of Mr and Mrs Hood
and their daughter,
Red Riding Hood.

While Mr Hood read the latest sports news, Mrs Hood
handed a basket to Red Riding Hood. It was filled with a
fruitcake, chocolate biscuits, jam tarts and a copy of
"Knitters' Weekly".
"Take this to your granny, dear," she said. "She's not very
well and this will cheer her up."
"OK, Mum," said Red Riding Hood, and off she went.

Tell your gran,
Rovers are top
dogs again.

Be careful, and
don't dawdle
in the woods.

OK, Mum.

Can I
have a
choccie
biccie?

A short time later, deep in Tangled Wood,
the Bears met Red Riding Hood scoffing jam tarts.
"Hello, Bears," she said, still munching. "I'm off
to see my granny – she isn't very well."
"Oh dear," said Mrs Bear. "Give her our love."
And they waved goodbye.
However, no one noticed
that hiding behind
the bushes, Big Bad
Wolf had heard
every word.

I'm all ears.

A few minutes later Big Bad Wolf met Jack on his paper round.

"Howdy, Jack," said Big Bad Wolf. "I'm off to visit Granny Hood, she's a bit poorly. Give me her newspaper and I'll take it for you."

It's on my way.

Great!

"OK, thanks," said Jack, and off he scooted. Moments later Big Bad Wolf knocked on the door of Granny's cottage.

"Who's there?" said Granny
in a small, shaky voice.
"It's the paperboy," Big Bad
Wolf fibbed. "I've got your
'Fairytale News'."

No sooner had Granny opened the
door than Big Bad Wolf leapt
inside and shoved poor
Granny into a cupboard.

Then Big Bad Wolf put on
Granny's spare bloomers
and nightie and hopped into her bed.

Big Bad Wolf made himself very
comfy and settled down to read
Granny's copy of the "Fairytale
News" while he waited for
little Red Riding Hood.

It wasn't very long before
Red Riding Hood arrived at Granny's
cottage and knocked on the door.
When she went inside she saw
a pair of big hairy ears poking
over the top of the newspaper.

Come in, dear.

"Oh! What big hairy ears you have, Granny,"
said Red Riding Hood.

"All the better to hear
you with, my dear,"
growled Big
Bad Wolf.

Red Riding
Hood stared
into Big Bad
Wolf's huge
eyes, gleaming
behind Granny's spectacles.

"Oh! What big eyes you have, Granny," she said.
"All the better to see you with, my dear,"
growled Big Bad Wolf, licking his lips.

"And – oh! What big teeth you have, Granny!" said Red
Riding Hood in a very wobbly voice.

"All the
better to EAT
you with!"
roared Big
Bad Wolf.

SUDDENLY the door crashed open!

There, filling the doorway, was Mr Hood. He'd popped round to Granny's with some wood for her fire.

"Oi! Wot's goin' on 'ere?"

he roared as he swung
his big axe.

Big Bad Wolf leapt straight out
of the window and ran off into the woods.

As he ran he passed Jack, who was very surprised
to see Big Bad Wolf in
Granny's clothing.

Meanwhile...

After their long walk
the Bears arrived back

at Honey Cottage to discover all was not as it should be.

"Someone's been eating my porridge!"
roared Mr Bear.

"Someone's been eating my porridge!"
growled Mrs Bear.

"And someone's been eating my porridge and eaten
it all up!" sobbed Baby Bear.

"Someone's been sitting in my chair!"

roared Mr Bear.

"Someone's been sitting in my chair!"
growled Mrs Bear.

"And someone's been sitting in my
chair and broken it!" sobbed Baby Bear.

"And what's that noise?" said Mr Bear.
"Sounds like someone's snoring," said
Mrs Bear, and they all dashed
upstairs to the bedroom.

ZZZZ

"Someone's been sleeping in my bed!"
roared Mr Bear.

"Someone's been sleeping in my bed!"
growled Mrs Bear.

"And someone's been sleeping in my bed, and they're still in it!" yelled Baby Bear.

All this roaring and growling woke Goldilocks.

"Eeek!" she screamed, and leapt out of bed and ran off!

Not far away, Jack was delivering his last copy of the "Fairytale News" – to his mum.

As Mrs Hubbard read the market news in the paper, she said, "Look, Jack, cows are selling well. Why don't you take Daisy to town and try to get a good price for her?"

We haven't got a penny to our name.

We're all washed-up.

So Jack set off for the market with Daisy. Along the way they met a fast-talking stranger, who said, *"I'll give you this magic bean for your fine cow, here and now. Whaddya say?"*

It's magic!

Pull the udder one.

"OK, done!" said Jack. He took the magic bean, and the fast-talking stranger took Daisy.

When Jack got home he gave his mum the magic bean. She was furious.

"You stupid boy," she roared. "You've been done!"
"But, but … it's a magic bean, Mum," stammered Jack.

"Magic bean? I'll give you magic bean!" said Jack's mum, throwing the bean out of the window.

"Look, it's disappeared!"

What a fairy story!

But it's magic, Mum.

It's bean and gone!

The next morning,
as Jack arrived back at Tumbledown
Cottage after his paper round,
he saw an enormous
beanstalk growing
in the garden.

"Wow!"
said Jack. "It was
a magic bean."
"Be careful," called
his mum, as Jack
began to climb the
beanstalk. Higher
and higher
he went,
until...

Eventually

he reached the top, where he found a
huge castle. Inside the castle lived a giant –
who, to Jack's horror, suddenly appeared, shouting,

"Fee, fi, fo, fum!"

Jack was so scared that he ran away to hide. But
as he did so, he dropped his mum's newspaper.

"Wot's this?"

said the giant, as he bent
down and picked up the
newspaper. He'd never seen
the "Fairytale News" before,
and once he started reading he became totally absorbed
in all the news. He was so fascinated that he didn't even
notice Jack stealing away
with his magic harp.

The next day ...

Jack climbed the beanstalk again, carrying another copy of the "Fairytale News".

Again, the giant appeared, shouting,

"Fee, fi, fo, fum!"

This time, however, as Jack ran away he dropped the newspaper on purpose. Again the giant picked it up, and again he didn't notice when Jack sneaked off with his hen that laid golden eggs.

The following day, up Jack climbed again.

This time, however, when the giant appeared, shouting,

"Fee, fi, fo, fum!"

he didn't stop to read the "Fairytale News"
but chased Jack and caught him!

"Gotcha!" boomed the giant at a terrified Jack. "You're the one 'oo's been pinchin' me stuff. So I'm going to eat you up! Unless ... you promise you'll climb up here every day with a copy of the 'Fairytale News'. Wotcha say?"

Jack agreed and was as good as his word. Every morning he climbed the beanstalk with a newspaper for the giant, who always gave Jack a golden sovereign and a mug of tea.

Jack and his mum became very rich, but Jack still delivered the "Fairytale News" to Beanstalk Castle, as he so enjoyed going to see his best friend the giant.

And, of course, they all lived happily ever after.

CHARLIE WAG ★ ANDREWSHOP
★ FAIRYLAND'S TOP NEWS ★

Fair...

BLACKBIRD ATTACK!

While the King was counting his
money and the Queen was eating a
honey sandwich, laundry maid Miss
Rose Garden was washing the clothes,
when, suddenly, down came a large
blackbird that pecked her on the nose.
The bird was thought to be one of
twenty-four that had escaped from a
sixpenny pie made by Simple Simon.
Dr Foster has put a vinegar and
brown paper plaster on Miss Garden's
nose and advised her to stay indoors.

NICK

BIG BA...

ARRESTED IN...

IT LOOKS AS THOUGH BB

oday, shortly after his r
from jail on bail. BB W
arrested yet again. BB
been in jail for blow
the Little Pigs' houses, this
accused of impersonating G
locking her in a cupboard
nightdress and, worst of
to eat up Little Red Ridi
BB Wolf was found w
nightdress, lacy nightg

IN

and see the fur flying

UDDERLY RIDICULOUS

It has been reported from Diddle
Diddle Farm that a cow has jumped
over the moon. At the scene we spoke
to a little dog, who laughed and said,
And a cat played the fiddle and
away with the spoon! You
thing that you

PROPERTY FOR SALE

e in need of
dy, but

Today